GW00888750

A DORLING KINDERSLEY BOOK

First American Edition, 1992
10 9 8 7 6 5 4 3 2 1
Published in the United States by Dorling Kindersley, Inc.,
232 Madison Avenue, New York, New York 10016

For Sam

ISBN 1-56458-105-5
Library of Congress Catalog Card Number 92-52801

Color reproduction by Dot Gradations
Printed in Singapore by Tien Wah Press Ltd

# Furry ANIMALS

Illustrated by
Kenneth Lilly

Written by
Angela Wilkes

DORLING KINDERSLEY, INC.

NEW YORK

# Contents

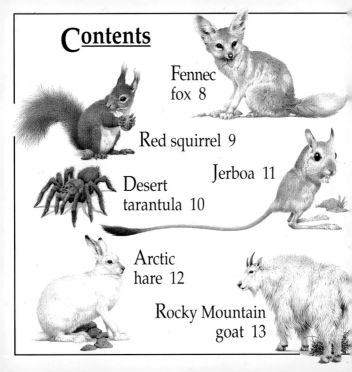

**Fennec fox**
The fennec fox lives in the hot desert. Its huge ears help keep it cool.

**Red squirrel**
The squirrel's long, bushy tail helps it balance as it leaps from tree to tree.

**Desert tarantula**
This huge, hairy spider hides away during the day, coming out only at night to hunt for food.

**Jerboa**
This desert rodent is like a tiny kangaroo. It can jump a long way to escape from its enemies.

**Arctic hare**
The Arctic hare's coat turns white in winter and brown in summer, to match its surroundings.

12

**Rocky Mountain goat**
This goat has long, shaggy fur to keep it warm on frigid mountain tops.

13

**Indri**
This bushy-
tailed lemur
wails loudly to warn
rival families to keep away.

14

## Giant panda
This rare bear wears a black "face mask" and feeds on bamboo shoots.

## Koala
Koalas live
high up in
treetops
and carry
their babies
wherever
they go.

16

**Duck-billed platypus**
This unusual animal is furry, but it has webbed feet and a bill like a duck.

17

**Brown bear**
This bear catches fish and digs up roots, shoots, and bulbs with its long claws.

18

**Leopard**
The leopard's spotted fur helps it slink unseen through trees and long grass.

19

**Musk ox**
This ox has very long, thick fur to keep it warm in the wind and snow.

# Where do the animals live?

**Fennec fox**
Sahara desert,
northern Africa

**Red squirrel**
European woodlands

**Desert tarantula**
North American deserts

**Jerboa**
Sahara desert,
northern Africa

**Arctic hare**
Arctic regions

**Rocky Mountain goat**
The Rocky Mountains,
North America

**Indri**
Madagascar

**Giant panda**
China

**Koala**
Australia

**Duck-billed platypus**
Australia

**Brown bear**
Northern Hemisphere

**Leopard**
African rain forests

**Musk ox**
Arctic regions

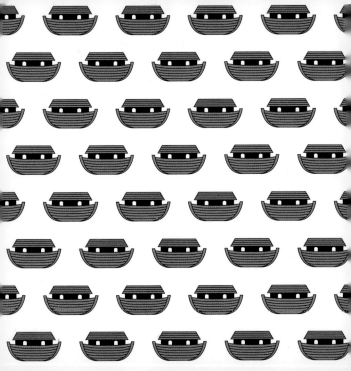